Bison

Grizzly Bear

Osprey

Bighorn Sheep

Red Squirrel

Mule Deer

Gray Wolf

Wrinklerump

By Marian Parks

Illustrated by Christine Karron

Near the old Fishing Bridge, on a knotty pine stump,
Sat a young grizzly bear fondly called Wrinklerump.
He pondered and worried as the day grew dark
How he'd survive winter in Yellowstone Park.

He was just two years old and not fully grown,
And had to plan for his first winter alone.
Like all grizzly bears he would need a safe den,
Where he'd hibernate until spring came again.

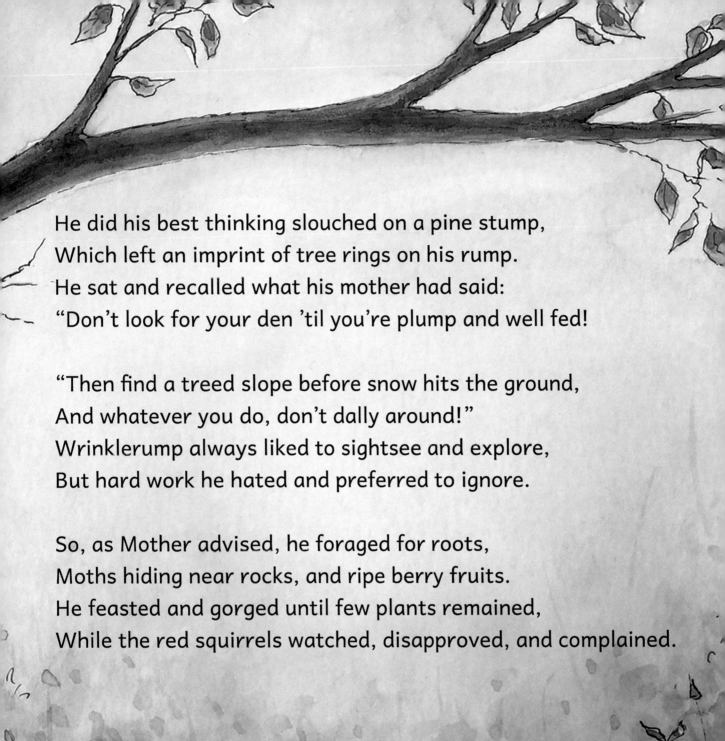

He did his best thinking slouched on a pine stump,
Which left an imprint of tree rings on his rump.
He sat and recalled what his mother had said:
"Don't look for your den 'til you're plump and well fed!

"Then find a treed slope before snow hits the ground,
And whatever you do, don't dally around!"
Wrinklerump always liked to sightsee and explore,
But hard work he hated and preferred to ignore.

So, as Mother advised, he foraged for roots,
Moths hiding near rocks, and ripe berry fruits.
He feasted and gorged until few plants remained,
While the red squirrels watched, disapproved, and complained.

Squirrel said, "Wrinklerump, are you aware,
That you've eaten far more than your rightful share?
If you stay much longer red squirrels will be doomed.
The twigs, seeds, and insects will all be consumed!

"We forage all winter—nearly starve until spring—
While you'll hibernate and not need a thing.
Please! Go down the river to claim your cave spot!
You'll find lots of fish and a cozy mud pot."

Feeling ashamed and a bit hungry, too,
He borrowed two oars and a wooden canoe.
Past LeHardys Rapids he found a mud pot
And sat down to munch on the trout that he'd caught.

A rotten-egg stench filled the air all around,
And mud pots burped gas from the piping-hot ground.
"That's sulfuric acid turning rock into goo,"
Announced Bison Bull, who lived there and knew.

"This place isn't safe," the old bison said.
"You should make your cave in the mountains ahead."
Then the hot springs sizzled! Gassy mud pots roared!
The bear ran for the boat and jumped safely aboard.

The broad Hayden Valley soon burst into view,
With mule deer and pronghorns gliding gracefully through.
"Where's everyone going?" Wrinklerump asked a deer.
She said, "Migrating south like we do every year.

"You should be in the mountains," scolded the doe,
"Most bears made their caves more than two weeks ago.
Head for the trees! They'll help hide your den."
But Wrinklerump paddled off downstream again.

Noisy white pelicans soared through the sky.
They also were leaving and honking goodbye.
Wrinklerump waved as they passed side by side
And then held on tight for a rollicking ride.

He raised his legs high for the Upper Falls treat
And squealed as he plunged over one hundred feet.
He was having fun and feeling carefree
And wanted more time to explore and sightsee.

He scampered to shore just before Lower Fall
And climbed right up Yellowstone's Grand Canyon wall.
Gas and steam puffed from the rhyolite crust,
Eroding the rocks and making them rust.

A lone osprey hovered above him and said,
"You'd better skedaddle. A storm is ahead."
The clouds in the sky loomed hostile and gray,
Which convinced Wrinklerump to leave right away.

Mount Washburn was close. He could see its treed side,
So he thought he had time for the Grand Loop bus ride.
He would hop off the bus at the Mount Washburn sign
And then look for a grove of spruce, aspen, or pine.

But the journey was bumpy, windy, and steep,
And lulled the young bear into a deep sleep.
The bus passed Mount Washburn and was now westward bound
To a place where a cave wouldn't likely be found.

At Mammoth Hot Springs Wrinklerump stirred awake,
Alarmed and upset at his foolish mistake.
This was no treed slope, but instead a strange mound
Rising like stairs from the steaming-hot ground.

"It's travertine rock," a perceptive elk said.
"It flows to the surface from the limestone seabed.
Cracks in the earth cause hot water to rise,
And what's left behind is this white stone surprise."

Wrinklerump thought, "Well, what should I do?
The travertine rock is too hard to dig through!"
Snowflakes now fell through the bitter cold air.
Wrinklerump knew he had no time to spare.

He lumbered for miles 'til he reached an odd stream
That billowed out puffs of foul-smelling steam.
"This is Firehole River," a moose bellowed out,
"Known for fumaroles and delightful brown trout.

"Fumaroles are gassy, rare thermal features.
Steam gushes from vents like lost, ghostly creatures.
Magma heats water that's seeped underground
And turns it to steam with a shrill, hissing sound."

"It's a grand river," Wrinklerump replied,
"But I need a den on a treed mountainside."
Wrinklerump shivered. Snow coated his snout.
He worried that maybe his time had run out!

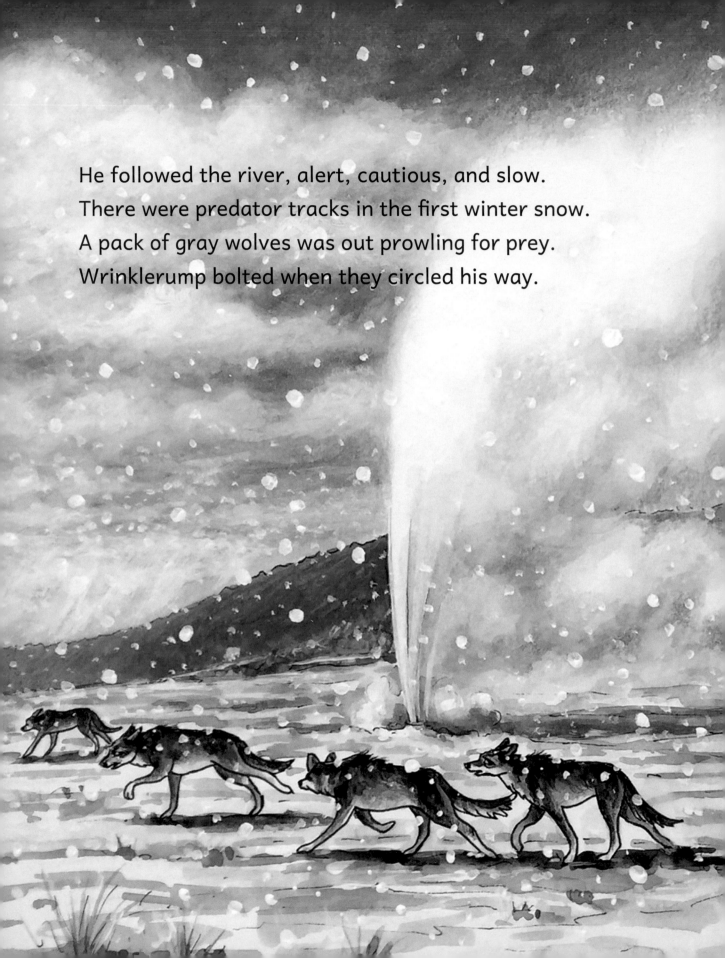

He followed the river, alert, cautious, and slow.
There were predator tracks in the first winter snow.
A pack of gray wolves was out prowling for prey.
Wrinklerump bolted when they circled his way.

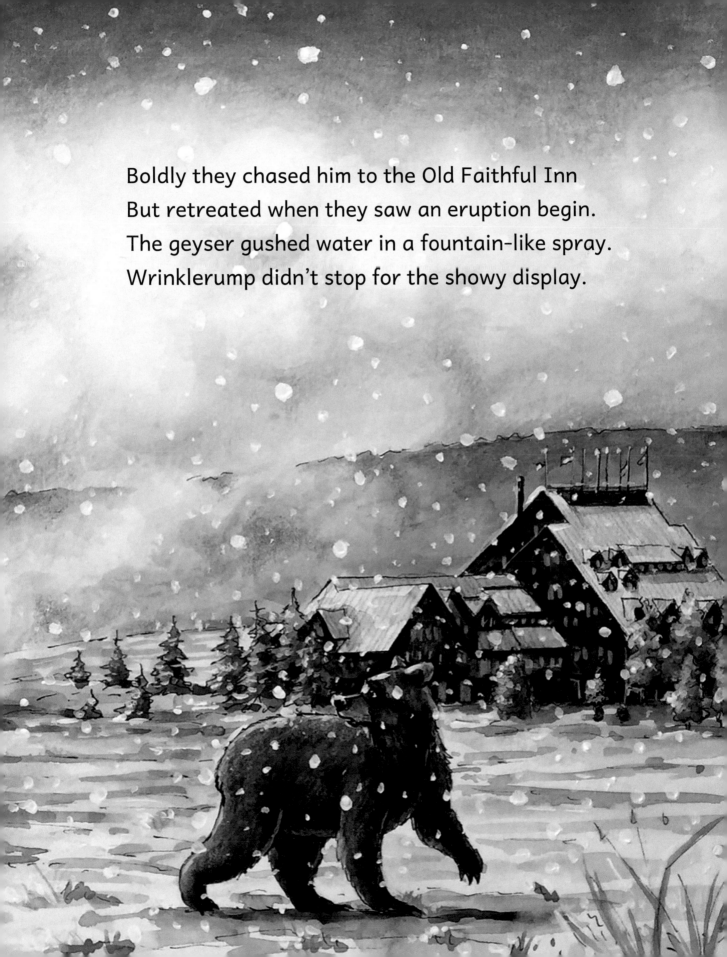

Boldly they chased him to the Old Faithful Inn
But retreated when they saw an eruption begin.
The geyser gushed water in a fountain-like spray.
Wrinklerump didn't stop for the showy display.

Plodding to Yellowstone Lake's icy shore,
He wondered if he could go on anymore.
Snow flurries were blinding. Wind pummeled his head.
Why hadn't he done as Mother had said?

"Don't dally around!" was what she'd always say.
"Wrinklerump, do your work, and then you can play."
He wished he had waited 'til spring to sightsee
And instead burrowed into a hollowed-out tree.

Wrinklerump slowly raised his frost-coated eyes.
It took him a moment to fully realize
That he'd reached Lake Village, near old Fishing Bridge,
And his favorite park trail with a view from the ridge.

The snowfall was easing when he found the trail sign
That led to a slope of spruce, aspen, and pine.
He trudged through deep snow, using muscle and might,
Toward the north side that was sheltered just right.

At the base of a tree he dug through the snow,
Making sure that his cave was hidden and low.
He made a small chamber without a front door
And then laid out spruce boughs for a bed on the floor.

He sat on a stump before going in
And thought of the magical places he'd been.
He relaxed, worry-free, alone in the dark,
Knowing he'd survive winter in Yellowstone Park.

For my Henry and Calvin
—M. P.

For Rene, my best friend and the love of my life
—Ch. K.

Nature Tale Books, Inc.
Livermore, California
www.NatureTaleBooks.com
Sales@NatureTaleBooks.com

LCCN: 2017911258

Summary: A young grizzly bear should be making his winter cave,
but the wonders of Yellowstone National Park distract him and
leave him unprepared for winter.

Story Themes: Earth Science | Self-discipline | Animals Prepare for Winter
| Yellowstone National Park

Hardcover ISBN: 9781943172030

Illustrations were created in watercolor, acrylic, colored pencil,
and ink by Christine Karron.

Printed in USA

10 9 8 7 6 5 4 3 2 1

Nature Tale Books

Visit our website for
Story Activities
www.NatureTaleBooks.com

Elk

White Pelican

Chipmunk

Pronghorn

Pika

Moose

Black Bear